KEEKER

and the Not-So-Sleepy Hollow

Text © 2008 by Hadley Higginson.
Illustrations © 2008 by Lisa Perrett.

Series design by Kristine Brogno and Mary Beth Fiorentino.
Book design by Mariana Oldenburg.
Typeset in Weiss Medium.
The illustrations in this book were rendered in Adobe Illustrator.
Manufactured in China.

Library of Congress Cataloging-in-Publication Data
Higginson, Hadley.
Keeker and the not-so-sleepy hollow / by Hadley Higginson ; illustrated by
Lisa Perrett.
p. cm.
Summary: Keeker and her parents take Plum the pony and Goatie the goat to
visit Keeker's aunt, uncle, and cousins in upstate New York, near the town of
Sleepy Hollow, the site of a famous scary story.
ISBN 978-0-8118-6074-1
[1. Ponies—Fiction. 2. Vacations—Fiction. 3. Family—Fiction. 4. New York
(State)—Fiction.]
I. Lisa Perrett, ill. II. Title.
PZ7.H53499Kecn 2008
[Fic]—dc22
2007003943

10 9 8 7 6 5 4 3 2 1

Chronicle Books LLC
680 Second Street, San Francisco, California 94107

www.chroniclekids.com

KEEKER

and the Not-So-Sleepy Hollow

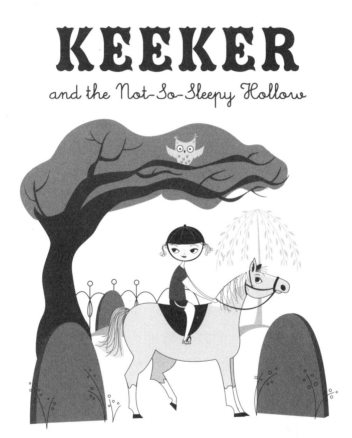

by **HADLEY HIGGINSON** Illustrated by **LISA PERRETT**

chronicle books · san francisco

Chapter 1

This is Catherine Corey Keegan Dana, but everyone calls her Keeker. Keeker is ten and a half. She lives in Vermont with her parents, five dogs, two cats, two horses, a goat, a bird, and a handful of woolly bear caterpillars. Keeker also has a pony, named Plum.

Everyone gets along very well with everyone. But Keeker and Plum are especially close.

In the summertime when it's too hot to go riding, Keeker and Plum like to go swimming.

In fact, there's a pond behind Keeker's house that's just right for cooling off. (It's mucky on the bottom but nice once you're in.)

Plum's favorite thing is to wade in belly-deep and paw and splash. Keeker likes to dog-paddle. She's also very good at squirting water through her teeth.

One particularly sticky day when Keeker and Plum had been down at the pond for hours, they heard a big ruckus coming from the house.

Keeker's mom was yelling and laughing, and someone else was talking really loudly.

Keeker hopped on Plum, and they sploshed out of the pond to see what was going on.

As it turned out, Uncle Mac was going on! Uncle Mac was Keeker's mom's sister's husband. He was in Vermont for business, and he had stopped by to say hello.

"Hi, Keeker!" said Uncle Mac. "You're getting gigantic! It's good to see you."

"I bet your kids are getting big, too," said Keeker's mom, to Uncle Mac. "How is everyone?

How's Marilee?" (Marilee was Mrs. Dana's sister.)

"They're great," said Uncle Mac. "In fact, that's kind of why I'm here. Marilee wanted me to ask you guys if you all wanted to come for a visit this summer. There's plenty of room. Even for ponies." He gave Keeker a little wink.

Keeker's uncle Mac and aunt Marilee and her cousins had just moved into a big old house. Keeker thought it would be fun to visit. Her mom did, too.

Keeker's mom clapped her hands. "YES!
We'd love that!"

"We've moved the horses to the new place,"
said Uncle Mac. "We probably have something
Keeker could ride. Or she could bring her own
pony. Like I said, plenty of room!"

"What? YEA!" Both Keeker and her mom
clapped and hopped.

Plum shuffled her feet grouchily. "Humph.
Summers are for lazing around and splashing in

the pond," she thought. "Why on earth would
anyone want to go anywhere?"

Keeker's dad looked as if he agreed with Plum.

"A five-hour drive WITH the horse trailer?"
said Keeker's dad. "I don't know—that is one
long haul!" He trotted off to his wood shop,
looking worried.

Keeker and her mom hurried after him.

"It really would be fun," said Keeker's mom.
"Plus, I haven't seen my sister in ages! I bet
Keeker doesn't remember what her cousins
look like. . . ."

That was a bit of an exaggeration: Keeker had seen her cousins two Christmases ago. She remembered exactly what her bossy cousin Vivi looked like (frizzy hair and braces). And Vivi's older brother, Ben, was kind of tall, with glasses that slid down his nose.

But it seemed to convince Keeker's dad.

"Oh, fine," he said with a gigantic sigh. "Road trip to New York!"

Chapter

2

The next couple of weeks whizzed by in a flurry of preparations. Suitcases had to be packed. The neighbor had to be called to see if she could take care of the other animals while the Danas were away. And of course, the horse trailer had to be cleaned out and made extra-comfy.

There was only one problem: Keeker's parents were afraid that Plum might get anxious on such a long trailer trip, riding all by herself.

"We could bring Goatie . . . ," suggested Keeker.

"That Goatie," thought Plum. "There is just no escaping her!"

It was settled. The Danas put their suitcases in the truck, loaded Plum and Goatie onto the trailer (with quite a lot of pushing and

pulling and carrot dangling), and off they went, heading west toward New York State.

Both Plum and Goatie had hay bags, to give them something to do during the long, boring trip. *Munch, munch*—the hay was quite tasty. In fact, the combination of the sweet hay and the gently swaying trailer was rather relaxing. Plum began to feel sleepy.

That is, until Goatie crawled under the bar and began to bug her. Goatie had eaten all her hay. Then Goatie had eaten her hay bag. Now Goatie was standing underneath Plum, nibbling gently on Plum's pony blanket.

Plum stamped her feet. "Go AWAY, Goatie!"

It was going to be a long drive. Plum could already tell.

Up in the truck, things weren't going much better. Keeker and her mom and dad were sick of playing "I spy." They were sick of singing songs. They were all bored to death of the drive to New York.

Plus, there wasn't much room.

"Keeker, shove OVER," said Keeker's mom, giving her a little push. "Your book is digging into my leg!"

"Mom, QUIT IT!" said Keeker, giving her mother a little poke.

"All right, you two!" said Mr. Dana.

When were they going to get there?

About nine zillion hours later (actually, about four hours and twenty minutes later), they pulled into a little town filled with big trees and pretty, old-fashioned houses. It seemed very peaceful.

"Lovely," said Keeker's mom happily. She liked old houses.

"I think we're almost there," said Keeker's dad. (He sounded pretty happy, too.)

They turned down a narrow street, and at the end of that street was a giant pink house that looked like a madman had built it. It had

shingles. It had turrets. It had gables and curli-cues. It was a crazy house!

"What kind of weirdos live THERE?" laughed Keeker.

Then she saw her very own uncle Mac out on the porch, waving hello. "Welcome!" he yelled.

Chapter 3

Uncle Mac led them around to the back of the house, where the stables were. Even the stables had turrets—crazy!

"Pretty fancy," thought Plum.

"It would be fun to play dress-up here," thought Keeker.

"That door looks tasty," thought Goatie.

Plum and Goatie had their own big stall to

share, right next to Vivi's pony, Bottle. Bottle
was shiny and black. Right next to Bottle was
another pony, Rocket, who was also shiny and
black. They looked a lot like twins.

"The ponies used to be a driving team," said
Uncle Mac. "They're a matched set. Cool,
right?"

"Or very strange and creepy," thought Plum. For once, she was glad to have Goatie around. She and Goatie stayed in one corner of their big stall so Plum could keep an eye on her weird cousins.

Bottle and Rocket just dozed. They didn't seem very interested in the visitors.

Inside the big, kooky house, everyone was talking and laughing and saying hello. Aunt Marilee made some sandwiches, and then Vivi

grabbed Keeker's arm and dragged her upstairs.
(Vivi was like that—very bossy.)

"So," said Vivi as soon as they were upstairs
in her room, "what do you think of this house?
It's TOTALLY haunted, you know. It's over a
hundred years old."

"Yikes," thought Keeker. It LOOKED like a

haunted house! There were even creepy old paintings of funny-looking people.

That night after dinner, Keeker and Vivi went upstairs to play "mystery sleuth." This was a game that Vivi had made up: Basically, all that happened was that Vivi and Keeker crept around with the lights turned off, hiding in closets and trying to scare each other. It was fun—for a little while.

"Enough of this made-up stuff," said Vivi. "I know a real mystery. Have you ever heard of the legend of Sleepy Hollow?"

"No," said Keeker.

"We learned about it in school," said Vivi. "In the Sleepy Hollow story, there's a ghost who's a horseman—a Headless Horseman! And he chases people through the woods. And he's just about the scariest thing ever."

Vivi took the flashlight and held it under her chin. "And guess what else," said Vivi in a creepy voice. "Right now we are very, very close to the village of Sleepy Hollow!"

Just then Vivi's brother, Ben, cracked open the bedroom door and stuck his head in.

"Mwah-ha-ha!" said Ben, making his favorite monster noise and holding his arms out like a zombie.

"Eeeeeeeeeek!" shrieked Keeker. She really
was pretty scared.

"Ben!" said Vivi. "Don't bug us." She wasn't
scared at all.

Out back in the old stables, Plum and
Goatie were having an unusual night, too. For

one thing, it was too quiet: Plum was used to hearing Pansy and Rosie shuffling around, and usually Rosie would poke her nose through the slats in the stall to say hello.

Bottle and Rocket didn't really shuffle, though—they just stood. Quietly, Plum peeked over her stall door, and there was Bottle looking right at her. Freaky!

Also, something was swooping around overhead. Something with big, wide wings.

"That had BETTER be a barn swallow," thought Plum nervously. But she had a sinking feeling it wasn't a barn swallow; it was a bat.

Plum tried to think about things that weren't scary: apples, groundhogs, carrots, and blue ribbons. It helped a little. She lay down in the corner of her stall. Goatie lay down right next to her, and Plum didn't even mind.

Chapter 4

The next day was sunny and hot. Even before breakfast was over, everyone felt sticky. Keeker's mom and Aunt Marilee were fanning themselves with the newspaper. Uncle Mac and Keeker's dad were flopped on the couch, talking about tractors. No one had much energy.

"It's way too hot to do anything but swim," whispered Vivi to Keeker. "Let's take the ponies and go to the lake! It's super fun!"

"Perfect!" whispered Keeker. How did Vivi know that was her absolutely favorite thing to do? Suddenly, Keeker's mom perked up a bit.

"This town is so historic," she said. "I think we should drive around and see some sites today. . . ."

Both Keeker and Vivi rolled their eyes and groaned. That was a terrible idea!

Fortunately, Vivi had a plan.

"Go and see sites with your mom, and we can go to the lake later on this afternoon. I'll get the ponies ready and get our bathing suits and stuff. Just meet me behind the barn as soon as you get back."

That was a great thing about bossy cousins. They were so well organized!

Keeker's mom bustled around getting maps and directions to all the historic sites.

"Where's your dad?" she asked Keeker. "Doesn't he want to come?"

Keeker's dad was hiding out in the basement with Uncle Mac. Very sneaky.

Keeker and her mom piled into the truck and headed into town. They looked at a bunch of old houses, an old church, and even an old mill. Keeker felt as if her eyeballs were going to

pop if she had to see even one more old thing.

"MOM," Keeker said, "Can we PUH-leeze go back? I'm supposed to meet up with Vivi."

"Don't you want to see Washington Irving's house?" asked her mom. "Washington Irving was a famous author who lived near here in the eighteen hundreds. He wrote a story called 'The Legend of Sleepy Hollow.'"

Sleepy Hollow! So it was true. Keeker decided one more site might not be so bad after all.

At Washington Irving's house, Keeker learned all about the Sleepy Hollow story. For one thing, she learned that the Headless Horseman was the ghost of a soldier who had lost his head in the Revolutionary War. According to the legend, he was haunting Sleepy Hollow as he tried to find it. ("Yikes," thought Keeker. She really didn't like the idea of someone roaming around looking for his head!)

She also learned that the person in the story who was most afraid of the Headless Horseman was a scaredy-cat schoolteacher whose name was Ichabod Crane.

"So did the horseman actually chase Ichabod or what?" asked Keeker.

"You'll have to read the story to find out," said her mom. "But let's just say that Ichabod had a very active imagination. . . ."

Chapter

5

After they left Washington Irving's house,
Keeker and her mom headed back to Vivi's. As
soon as they got there, Keeker raced out to
the barn, where Vivi and Bottle and Plum were
waiting for her. Vivi had thought of everything:
She had bathing suits, towels, even snacks.

"You're late," said Vivi sniffily. "It's almost five
o'clock!"

"Sorry! At least it's still hot," Keeker pointed out. Which was true. Even Plum was desperate to go swimming. She'd been standing in the sun with Keeker's bossy cousin FOREVER. She couldn't wait to splash around and cool off.

The four of them headed down the path into the woods, where they found a little road that was nothing more than two tracks with grass growing in the middle.

"This was the old stagecoach route," said Vivi bossily. She then proceeded to tell Keeker all kinds of boring facts about stagecoaches and horse carriages and how people used to deliver the mail about a zillion years ago.

Fortunately, Keeker was riding behind Vivi so she didn't really have to pay attention. While Vivi blah-blahed, Keeker looked around at all the big old trees and the ferns and the crumbly stone walls. It looked a lot like home. It was nice!

Plum kept an eye on Bottle's shiny black rump. She still didn't trust that weird twinsy pony. . . .

After they'd clomped along for about half an hour, the stagecoach road seemed to end. There was a cemetery on their right, and straight ahead was town, with bigger roads and cars.

"Hmmmm," said Vivi. "You know, I haven't actually ridden to the lake in a long time. I usually go in the car with my dad."

For once, Vivi looked a little unsure of herself.

"Well," said Keeker, "we can't go through town because there are cars."

"I know—duh," said Vivi. "Let's cut through the cemetery instead. See that gravel road? If we go down there past the church, I think we'll come out near the lake."

Keeker wasn't sure. But Vivi was the boss. So off they went, with Bottle leading the way.

On the far side of the church, the gravel road continued into a small patch of woods. Bottle and Plum stopped, peering suspiciously into the tangle of dark, scraggly trees. Vivi clucked at Bottle.

"Let's keep going," she said. "I really want to go swimming, don't you? Plus, we've come this far. C'mon."

Keeker wasn't so sure. The woods reminded

her of the Sleepy Hollow story. "It's getting so late . . . ," said Keeker.

"Don't be a baby," said Vivi.

They kept going.

Inside the woods, it was dim and quiet. The trees seemed to press in toward them as they rode by. And even though they were close to town, they couldn't hear a single car.

Plum stayed right behind Bottle. They went farther. And it got darker.

Something swooped across the road in front of them.

A branch brushed Plum's ears. "BAT!" thought Plum. She was glad no one could see that her eyes were bugging out.

Then—even SCARIER—they heard a shuffling noise behind them. Both ponies wheeled around and saw something standing in the road. Something with four legs—and a lumpy-looking rider.

"Headless HORSEMAN!" shrieked Keeker. (She couldn't help it—it was so scary!) She and Plum took off as fast as they could down the dark road. But Vivi didn't follow her. Vivi and Bottle just stood there looking at the thing in the road.

"Is that Rocket?" thought Bottle.

"Is that my BROTHER?" said Vivi. "Keeker, come back. It's just Ben trying to scare us!"

"WHAT?!" said Keeker, wheeling Plum back around again. "That's SO obnoxious!"

"Let's get him!" said Vivi.

"Mmmmwah-ha-ha!" yelled Keeker, doing her own version of the scary-monster noise. Now they'd see who was a baby!

Vivi and Keeker and Bottle and Plum chased the Headless Horseman all the way back through the cemetery.

Chapter
6

Ben was the first one to pull up. Rocket was
huffing and puffing, and Ben's face was red
and sweaty.

"Wow," he said. "You didn't have to chase me
like that. I was just kidding around!"

"Well, you scared us!" said Vivi. Her hair
looked extra-frizzy. She was still mad.

Keeker pretended to be mad, too. But secretly she thought it had been fun.

The only problem was that now it was REALLY late—almost suppertime.

"We'd better get back," said Ben. "Every-one's gonna be wondering where we are. You two must have been riding in circles, because you've been gone FOREVER but you weren't

very far away! I'm sorry you couldn't go swimming. But you know we could set the sprinklers
up on the lawn. . . ."

What a great idea! They rode back to the
house, laughing the whole way about how

silly Ben looked in his headless costume. Bats swooped, and owls hooted—but Keeker and Vivi were giggling so much they barely noticed.

When they got home, Keeker and Vivi told their parents all about the adventure in

the woods. (Ben got in a little bit of trouble,
but not much.) Then Uncle Mac set up the
sprinkler, and they all took turns running
through the water, and even riding through on
the ponies.

"Tickles!" snorted Plum as she and Keeker
charged through. But really it felt wonderfully
cool and delicious. Even Goatie took a turn!

That night Aunt Marilee made ice cream
in her old-fashioned ice-cream maker. The
grown-ups sat and talked about summery
things, and Keeker and Vivi fell fast asleep on
the sofa, snoring away, still in their bathing
suits.

Out in the stable, Plum and Bottle and
Rocket were enjoying a delicious dinner of
oats and apples while Goatie munched happily
on the Headless Horseman. (It was made of
cardboard—yum.)

The cool moon hung like a lamp in the big, dark sky. And the little town close to Sleepy Hollow got sleepier and sleepier. And finally fell fast asleep. *Zzzzz.*

Hadley Higginson grew up on a farm in Vermont where she had a sneaky pony of her own. She currently lives in Roanoke, Virginia, where she works as a freelance writer.

She no longer has a sneaky pony, but she does have a horse named Robbie and a bossy little dog.

To host an event with the author of this book, please contact publicity@chroniclebooks.com.